A Splendid Christmas

Christa Arnet

A Splendid Christmas

Thirteen Quirky Stories
from Switzerland

Second edition

Translated from German into English by Järvi Kotkas
and reviewed by Darren L. Pain

Illustrations by Järvi Kotkas

Bibliografische Information der Deutschen Nationalbibliothek: Die Deutsche Nationalbibliothek verzeichnet diese Publikation in der Deutschen Nationalbibliografie; detaillierte bibliografische Daten sind im Internet über dnb.dnb.de abrufbar.

First Printing: 2002, Christa Arnet „Die perfekte Weihnachtsfeier. Zwölf Weihnachtsgeschichten zum Schmunzeln"
© 2021 Christa Arnet "Die perfekte Weihnachtsfeier. Dreizehn Weihnachtsgeschichten zum Schmunzeln"
ISBN: 9-783752-617924

Illustrations: © 2021 Järvi Kotkas

Translation into English: © 2021 Järvi Kotkas

Herstellung und Verlag: BoD – Books on Demand, Norderstedt

ISBN: 978-3-7543-5556-5

Sincere thanks to my family, my friends and allies for having inspired me to write these tales.

Very special thanks to Järvi Kotkas for the skilful translations and technical support.

Table of contents

Christmas All-Year Round

My sister Susanne is a wonderful lady. She is a perfect wife, perfect mother, child-raiser, host, organiser, book-keeper, piano player and cook. Her ironed tablecloths are silky smooth, her garden paths are spotlessly clean and her kids, of course, are the best in the class. On top of that, she is punctual to a T. As long as I can remember, she has never been one minute late. She has never postponed a job from today to tomorrow, quite the opposite: whatever could be done tomorrow, is more often done yesterday. Her tireless discipline allows her to be done with the washing one day ahead of the official washing day, pack the bags a week ahead of holidays and lay the table a day before hosting.

Hence, it is fully understandable that she used to celebrate Christmas already on the 19th of December in order to – as she said – „be ahead in the race" and be able to spend the actual holidays in a more relaxed atmosphere. In the same vein, we found it completely reasonable to bring the celebration forward to the first Advent. In the beginning, some of the elderly aunts were taken aback and shook their heads, but soon they also recognised that this would help avoid the usual clashes of the year-end wrap-up and parties as well as the related headaches and upset tummies. Additionally, this brought along an upside that the gifts could be exchanged well ahead of the 24th.

However, the idea to start the celebrations already in November was novel and somewhat surprising even for us pragmatists. What brought everybody onside was Susanne's argument that there is a much bigger choice of gifts in the autumn and the prices are also much lower. In the end, isn't tinsel already glittering in every shopwindow by that time, isn't the house inundated with Christmas flyers and aren´t streetlights done up as a starlight show? If it is OK for a department store or street lighting, it is also alright for my sister: on 10th of November, the Christmas tree lights went on.

Having said that, it did not stay at November for long. The following year we were told that the celebration would be in September. My sister's family planned to head south for the autumn holidays and therefore would have no time to take on the Christmas preparations in October. We should respectfully understand this and appreciate that this little advance will increase the headstart for the official Christmas by another two months, which would certainly please all family members.

In spite of these undoubtedly noteworthy reasons we were a little bit disappointed at the beginning. The aunties were not the only ones looking forward to the 10th of November. Still, there was some comfort in the prospect of the forthcoming Advent season with its oldie afternoons, anniversaries in nursing homes, jumble sales, bowling nights and club meetings. So everyone arrived on the 14th of September at Susanne's beautiful home, to attend a fancy little party that was only disturbed by the noise of the roller-coasters, merry-go-rounds and shooting ranges from the nearby village fête happening at the same time.

***

For my sister, September remained the preferred Christmas season for some years. However, all of a sudden she replaced it with June. The advance was necessary, she explained, because it is best to buy the gifts in the summer sale and it makes no sense to hide them for weeks. It makes much more sense to celebrate shortly before the summer holidays and then recover from the Christmas stress at the seaside.

These arguments were of course convincing. What careful planning and perceptive thinking! Now we could admit that we always did buy a towel for Susanne and rubber fins for the lovely kids in June when bargain bins and discounted prices screamed for attention.

The June parties were consequently a big success, at least in the beginning. As time passed, it became clear that this arrangement had also certain disadvantages. Above all, it was difficult to get hold of marzipan angels, let alone snowflakes. Oddly enough, the self-made gingerbreads tasted a bit gluey as well. Most unpleasant of all however, was the rude laughter of the neighbours as we sat on the balcony decorated with candles during mild evenings and sang Silent Night.

After a lengthy family board meeting it was finally decided to set the headstart to mid-March, a date that was generally considered to be favourable because it lay in a holiday-free period between Easter and Carnival.

Indeed, March was such a perfect match that one could start wondering why other people hadn't come to the same idea earlier. Wintery surroundings offered a stylish background. Self-made gingerbreads stayed delightfully fresh, one could get sparklers in the Boxing Day sales and gifts in the January sales.

In short, March was as good as December.

Imagine then how annoyed we were when my sister suddenly abandoned March and brought the party forward to the 24th of December. Once we had understood the rationale, the penny dropped: what a wonderful idea to celebrate Christmas at Christmas! Enjoying the glittering starlight show from streetlights, buying marzipan angels on a whim and at times seeing snowflakes through the window!

***

So, this year we will – slightly awkward and unsure but full of good will – sit all together on Christmas Eve and hold a quiet little party free of merry-go-round music and neighbours' gleeful laughter. Like returning to a totally normal conventional life? Oh, no. Ours is fundamentally different from all other peoples´ and this gives us deep satisfaction: the blissful knowledge that we are an entire year ahead!

It Happened in Wullheim

The first person to hear about it was the editor of Wullheim Chronicle. The phone rang in the editor's office on Thursday night, shortly before 6pm. Kunz already had his coat on, needed a drink and was not particularly keen to field more complaints from angry readers. He had spent the entire day struggling with calls because of the article „Dog tax will increase" about the Wullheim township meeting that should have read „Dog tax will not increase". Just a typo, as happens every now and then.

But the phone rang so persistently that Kunz´s conscience and curiosity won out and he sat down again. Perhaps it was not a dog owner this time, and maybe there was something really interesting to deal with after all, like a fire, a murder, a burglary or a political sex scandal. An editor of a local newspaper must never give up hope.

As a matter of fact, it was not a dog owner. But the story was not particularly exciting either. Some baby had been born in a garage. Just like that, without any complications, perfectly healthy. Italians passing through, meh! As if this would be of any interest to Wullheim!

Kunz sighed, buttoned up his coat and headed to the nearby pub „Kreuz" for a wheat beer.

***

As it happened, that same evening Chief Inspector Schreiber was also sitting in the pub trying – as he put it – to get over an annoying matter. Shortly before 5pm, a suspicious couple with a newborn baby were spotted in a garage in Zutt-street. He – a worker, she – a waitress, both Italian, travelling from Germany.

According to the interview log, the two had asked for a room in „Sternen", but were turned away. The owner of the hotel explained that upon seeing them he was struck by a „funny feeling". Furthermore, he did not approve of home births, not least because of third-party liability and so on. In any case, he had no desire for something like that in his freshly renovated rooms. He had advised them to visit the municipal hospital.

„Of all things," grumbled Schreiber, „this happens always shortly before my shift is over."

„And where are these people now?", asked Kunz, who started to get wind of a possible story.

„For the time being, still in the garage", said Schreiber and took a long sip from his glass, „it's fine for them. Everything they need, is there. Blankets, mattresses, an electric oven, water and a toilet just nearby in the hobby-room. However, they must be gone tomorrow or the day after, at the very latest the day after that."

Then he gave a stern look at Kunz: „Mind you, do not write all of that in your paper if you want to stay out of trouble. Understood?"

„I understand", Kunz nodded. He knew it was better not to joke around with Schreiber.

Consequently, there was only a short piece in the „Nutshell" column of the next edition of the Wullheim Chronicle:

Wullheim, 21 December: On Thursday, a young Italian woman gave birth to a son in a garage. Maria (21) and Giuseppe (25) were on their travels from Germany, when she suddenly went into labour. According to eyewitnesses, they barely made it to the next garage before the baby arrived. Both the mother and the baby are well. Congratulations.

***

Let's go back to the Chief Inspector Schreiber. He had just arrived home, looking forward to enjoying the well-earned plate of Cervelat-Gruyère strips followed by a TV evening when the phone went off. A resident of Zutt-street insisted on receiving police help. She had been to the post office already and now she wanted to inform the Chief Inspector personally. What was happening in Zutt-street was absolutely preposterous for a normal person like herself. The streetlamps, eleven in total, were getting brighter and brighter by the hour. Of course, she knew exactly what she was talking about! It was now so bright that you could read a book outside. Like daylight! Like daylight! You couldn't even think about going to sleep.

Even the dog had not been able to sleep. Would the police be willing and able to protect the population from such technology glitches? Schreiber encouraged, soothed, protested, gave promises..., but then blew up and said things that are better not repeated here.

„Albert, don´t get upset", hushed his wife, „think about the upcoming Christmas." She should not have said that.

Schreiber yelled at her, all red in the face: „I will get upset any time I want!" His unmistakable, heavily-trained police intuition told him that this was only the beginning.

***

If truth be told, the police did not remain idle, even if it might have looked like that to outsiders. It wasn't for nothing, that the Wullheim Police Force were widely known for their great care and attention to detail. Two officers and a patrol car were dispatched without a delay to restore order. First things first, they confirmed it was very bright indeed. „Like in Worzstadt stadium", they both agreed.

Second, they tried to locate some representatives of the power plant or at least the key to the central switch in order to turn the annoying lights off. Unfortunately without result, since all the staff had already left for holidays without leaving anyone to replace them (which came to have repercussions, of course). To effect an immediate remedy, two police officers ordered that all houses roll down their blinds and if needed also draw the curtains. Corrective measures would be put in place the next morning.

***

However, the next morning the police had other things to do. There was the traditional Christmas market in the school courtyard. The area needed to be blocked off, instructions given to the market goers, licenses checked and permits stamped.

Already ten past nine, shortly after the market opened, the importance and urgency of the presence of law enforcement became evident. Without asking, someone had crept in and placed two rough boxes between Messmer Delicatessen and Klosswanger Wooden Goods, in preparation for spreading some dubious flyers.

It was Messmer who had brought this rude behaviour to the attention of the police. He might have had good reason to be concerned about the appeal of quince cookies, delicately decorated with Christmas ornaments, and highly-popular marzipan baby-Jesuses. Klosswanger had also a feeling that sales of the elegantly hand-carved angels might suffer. After all, he had lovingly decorated the stand with spruce sprigs, candles and baubles and it was only reasonable to expect decent neighbours.

Chief Inspector Schreiber who was there in person, recognised immediately that this thin, pale, long-haired figure in a baggy coat was out of place in Wullheim, let alone in the cheerful and well-organised hustle and bustle of the Wullheim Christmas market. Fortunately, he was well versed in handling such characters and the boxes were quickly removed. The man was banished from the square and the goods were confiscated. By the way, there was nothing of value, merely leaflets, roughly 2000 pieces.

Before Schreiber placed these in the police vault, to be used eventually as evidence, he had a quick look. „REJOICE, REJOICE", it read, „THE KING WAS BORN IN WULLHEIM."

„What rubbish", muttered Schreiber, feeling good that he had acted in a timely manner.

Meanwhile, the pale man caused another unpleasant incident. In the afternoon, just when the snow had gently started to fall, he appeared suddenly in "Kreuz", at the time when everyone was recovering from the shopping spree, having coffee and other pick-me-ups. Instead of humbly sitting down on a wooden bench next to the door he went straight to the regulars' table, planted himself in front of the perplexed members of the Wullheim Seniors-Club and chanted in a loud and shrill pitch: „Rejoice, rejoice, the king has arrived! Let's go to Zutt-street and celebrate together!"

„That one must be pissed," noted the pub-owner dryly and the regulars laughed. Before the intruder could say anything else, Haslinger and Schweingruber stood up, grabbed him by his coat sleeves and shoved him towards the door: „Come here, little one, this is the way to your king!"

The pub-owner shook his head: "Five o'clock in the afternoon and already two sheets to the wind."

***

It had been snowing all the night and in the morning dawn Wullheim was a picture of peace, covered in a big white blanket.

20

However, the look was deceiving. It was brewing under the surface. The residents of Zutt-street had had a bad night because the streetlamps were still glowing extraordinarily – „even more than during the first night", stressed many of the Zutt-streeters. Since the police so far had not worked out any solution, they decided to write an open letter to the city mayor. The text was roughly as follows:

Honourable Mr President!

When will our concerns finally be acknowledged? It looks like the authorities are asleep. We, however, cannot sleep! This unbearable light makes us sick. In addition, our Christmas celebrations are at risk. How can our Christmas lights stand out when it is plain daylight outside? In our opinion: everyone has the right to have Christmas! Including us in Zutt-street. In the absence of an official response, we will take things into our own hands.

Signed: residents of Zutt-street.

The President, however, already had enough on his plate. The short column in Wullheim Chronicle had made unexpected and most unpleasant waves. Both Women's Weekly as well as Worzstadt Observer had called the town hall inquiring about the details of the „garage birth". A reporter from the local radio station had even requested an interview, which could be rejected on the grounds that Mister President was busy that entire morning working on his Christmas address.

As a matter of fact, he sat at his desk staring gloomily at the letter from the Service Staff Union of the Wullheim county. They were scathing about the "disrespectful attitude towards a female representative of the profession" and demanded an immediate official position on the case of Maria S. Or else, they would find it necessary to reconsider supporting the President in the next election.

That took the biscuit. The matter with the baby had to be settled right away.

Chief Inspector Schreiber was called in and briefed about the latest developments. The President gave Schreiber a stern look: „This incident could damage Wullheim really badly, especially now when our application for the subsidy for the bypass road depends on the regional government. I am therefore tasking you with the welfare of our lovely town. Please make sure these immigrant workers disappear. Clear them out by noon."

He leant back in the leather armchair and lit a cigar: "Let the Wullheim Police service prove for once what it is capable of".

The rest can be told quickly since events started to unfold rapidly.

Schreiber was just on the way out, to order an inconspicuous patrol (in a grey police car), when the receptionist brought in a petition signed by the 86 Zutt-streeters. The President was in the middle of reading it when there was another knock on the door. „What the hell is wrong again?" he shouted peevishly. The receptionist came in timidly. Apparently three gentlemen had arrived, from afar. May-be he could be so kind as to…

The President hesitated: „Something is not quite right here. I guess it reminds me of something?"

He struggled getting to his feet and looked out of the window. Three black limousines were parked in front of the town hall, each with a chauffeur in a crisp uniform.

Then suddenly it dawned on him. The baby in the garage, the bright light in Zutt-street, three noble men from abroad…

„My God," he exclaimed, „could this really be true!?"

Just imagine what it would mean and what opportunities it would open up. Both for Wullheim and for him personally. What a stroke of luck – Wullheim as the centre of the world and he himself the President. Millions of visitors, millions to be cashed in. Repayment of debt, tax rate reduction, hotels, real estate property, villas. Obviously a new sports stadium, an amusement park, maybe a new town hall, certainly more car parks and a big shopping centre.

„Where is Schreiber?" he shouted into the waiting room, „Get Schreiber here now!"

It seemed an eternity until Schreiber arrived. When he finally stepped in, the President grabbed him by his tie: „The baby! The baby! Where is the baby?"

Schreiber first gave him a puzzled look, but then broke into a broad smile: „No worries, everything is taken care of. The baby is gone."

„What?" shrieked the President, „gone? Are you telling me – gone? Do you understand what it means for us, for Wullheim, for the entire world?" The sweat appeared in pearls along his forehead and he started shaking all over. „The baby must be found immediately. I say, immediately. Or else it will be a catastrophe."

Schreiber did not quite get it, but he understood that it sounded serious. Two men were dispatched in a patrol car, another one followed on a motor bike. First they went to Zutt-street, then they searched the entire block and finally they combed through the entire town. The volunteer fire department was engaged at two o'clock, by half past two the streets were blocked off and by three, cadets received a call to join the search. But all efforts remained futile.

The baby had disappeared.

***

There is nothing much else to say. Just that the President had a heart attack, which happened shortly after he had summarily fired Schreiber. Anyhow, Zutt-street was peaceful again, since from then on the streetlamps were shining as usual. The next evening, Wullheimers celebrated their undisturbed Christmas.

Everything was back to normal.

The Wish „Pusher"

All right, now that Christmas has once again arrived, I can reveal something to you. I am the one who is whispering the names of the newest perfume scents from behind the marble pillars of the opulent consumer temples, humming „salami" and „whisky" under my breath against the background music in department stores and chirping „Mama" in the doll section as well as making „choo-choo" sounds near toy trains. What I want to say is, it is not me in person but my recorded voice. At times it is loud, then again soft. At times it can be gently enticing, another time purring and erotic. Sometimes it takes on a cool style or joyous humour. However, this targeted, irresistible undertone will open people's eyes and hearts to what they absolutely must have for Christmas. As you might have guessed by now, my job is a wish „pusher".

***

My task requires of course, utmost subtlety. It is not for nothing that I studied five terms of psychology and four terms of philosophy, completed social work training and graduated from a hypnosis course. You have no idea how meticulously I must choose my tone and wording to avoid the risk of tempting people to a tea instead of a coffee, or even worse, filling them with enthusiasm for hair curlers instead of electric shavers.

Pushing a wish for salmon or skiing during Advent season is of course, a piece of cake. The real challenge is to plant an idea for inflatable mattresses or lawn mowers in November into the minds of men or possibly women. I often use the so-called billiard-effect, a method that I myself developed during night-long studies, which helps to achieve the goal with a carefully planned diversion. In order to sell fitness holidays, I first promote the sale of chocolates; in order to create the desire for chocolates, I first entice people to buy TVs or video players.

It may also happen that I have to handle cases which go beyond mere words and change completely the essence of a product. Take for example, the episode with yellow wool bobbles. Their intended use was to decorate slippers, but my client could get hold of them at bargain prices after a bankruptcy of a slipper producer. So it was my task to find a marketing idea, where I can humbly confirm, I had supreme success. I mixed the bobbles with baubles and played the sound of shattering glass hitting the floor every now and then during the silent night melody. The effect was astounding: every third customer took home yellow bobbles instead of Christmas tree baubles and one DIY journal even gave the first prize to the tree that was decorated with my bobbles. Ever since, there has been no drop-off in demand for these charming products.

***

My work normally begins in October when there are relatively few signs of Christmas. At that time, it will certainly be less about prompting impulse buying and more about long-term measures – preparing receptive grounds that will later, figuratively speaking, suck gratefully up all attacks via store catalogues and adverts. I become more decisive as of mid-November when I start discreetly spreading ideas in trams, trains, cinemas and restaurants. Only after the first of December is it going to be the full mind control and active directing behind the scenes.

***

However, my job is far from complete when soundtracks have been installed and programmed. What follows is the checking and performance review. With due regard to the surroundings, putting on a worried face and carrying multiple plastic bags, I mingle with the crowd and drift from one department store to the other, from the delicatessen to jewellery shop, from a book store to a fashion boutique. I might stop for a while at busy spots observing the reactions of people. Most of the time everything goes smoothly. My cautiously whispered „Mozart" energises the sale of lace blouses and my hearty laughter triggers everyone to grab the latest joke book. The sound of a ringing phone at the perfume stands inevitably makes male customers think about their secretaries, spouses or mothers and they will make animated requests for a perfume, night cream or wrinkle concealer. Even my carefully trained groaning is well placed: dozens of massage devices called „No more rheumatism" will get sold. Most touching to watch are young mothers when they reach out for teddy bears upon hearing my impression of a toddler sobbing. Then I go home, proud of myself, sit down in my rocking chair and contemplate new tactics in my half-sleep. I myself have understandably no Christmas wishes.

***

Years pass, one Christmas comes after the other. My methods become more refined and the overall increase in turnover is clearly measurable. There are hardly any hiccups. Only once, just one single time, I got briefly into trouble. I remember it clearly: it happened next to the scarves from the Far East that had been re-ordered already twice thanks to my expert coughing-soundtrack.

„Is this Christmas at all any more", said a voice next to me, „this uncharitable profiteering?"

The voice came from a pale man in a light-coloured robe.

I smiled at him gently. „My son," I replied, „Christmas is the time for presents. No presents, no Christmas."

I was about to head off but the man did not let me and started to blabber about some kind of earlier times with a serious face. He suggested Christmas had had a completely different meaning in those days. It was something concerning peace and love. I wanted to shake my head and explain to him that giving presents is exactly about love. However, I was suddenly facing a peculiar force and the words got stuck in my throat. It looked as if this force radiated all over his face and body and wrapped him into an intense bright light.

I must have been sort of mentally deranged, because this is the only way I can explain what followed.

Suddenly I saw the spree of wishes and shopping that I had fuelled flash before my eyes as a sequence of a few key movements. Robot-like people stormed at me from every direction and on their way they grabbed goods from the surrounding shelves and tossed them at me, or to be precise into me - because I had turned into a big plastic bag.

I started to feel dizzy and at the same time I experienced an unfamiliar feeling – I had a wish. I had a very specific, scandalous wish: „Would these wretched soundtracks just shut up!"

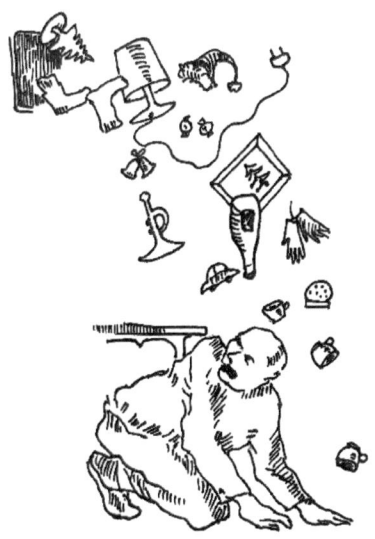

„Much better," said the man next to me. In a blur, I saw him giving me a friendly nod while I was coughing, gasping and holding on to scarves.

I had expected the world to end which, however, did not happen. Fortunately, my eyesight came back to normal and I recognised gratefully that all was still as it used to be: bustling and money-making.

A baby's voice was sobbing behind the teddy bears, the telephone rang next to the perfumes and my groaning brought life to the massage devices. In a few minutes I was again my old self. I rushed back home, looking forward to recording my new whisper. My intended message was crystal clear, next year my syrupy voice would announce: „Peace and happiness" between the sugar angels and garden gnomes.

Appalling Behaviour

As a matter of fact, we have known Mr Gantenbein for a long time. He lives a short distance from us, in an ordinary, old house at the end of the street. He drives past our house twice on workdays, from left to right in the morning and from right to left in the evening. Saturdays and Sundays he passes by on foot, but nobody knows from where he comes or where he goes. He is always in a hurry, hardly offering more than a „Good Day" or „Good Evening".

For the first ten years of being neighbours, we did not really pay much attention to him and he did not give us much reason to either. Judging by his earnest face, black briefcase and pin dot tie, we thought he was a civil servant or a bank employee of high rank. In short, a serious man with a serious job, anything but a day dreamer.

Yet, we were fools, or rather he let us be fooled! Four years ago, just before Christmas, it became clear that we knew next to nothing about the real Gantenbein. We had been living all this time close to a wolf in sheep's clothing or perhaps a sheep in wolf's clothing.

***

I can still very well remember those turbulent days of Advent. The widow Meyer from the neighbouring house was the first one affected. On the 13th of December, a small parcel was delivered to her, stating Walter Gantenbein as the sender. You can well imagine that Mrs Meyer was quite surprised indeed. After all, she had never had any business with Gantenbein. Her surprise was even greater when she opened the parcel: it contained a brand-new coin made of pure gold!

Mrs Meyer swallowed dryly, sat down and rubbed her eyes. At the same time her mind was weighing an array of possible uses for the present. Soon however, doubts started to stir, turning quickly into irritation. How could that Gantenbein come to the idea to send her a gold coin? Was he making a clumsy advance? Had she perhaps given him any reason for closer contact? Maybe it was some form of bribery? Or maybe he believed she was in need of financial support? All the same, before she had reached any conclusion, she discovered that Mrs Schutz and Mrs Lattmann had also been honoured with gold coins. The following days the Roggenmosers, Nussbaumers, Itens and Pfisters found similar parcels in their mailboxes. By the 20th of December, the entire neighbourhood had gotten Gantenbein's gold, including us. That was not all however, there were rumours in the village that each and every postman, street cleaner, policeman and child minder had received the present.

***

Even though everyone was rushed off their feet preparing for Christmas and unexpected fuss was absolutely not welcome, a community meeting was convened in the small dining room of the restaurant "Sonne". In the end, it was necessary to agree on a harmonised approach, right? Given the urgency of the matter, almost everyone who had been affected took part and a lively discussion got going under the leadership of Salomon Kraut, a qualified gardener and the president of the Singing Club. It was crystal clear that no sane person would give such presents and if they did then only with some ulterior motive. But what could that be? Did he want to buy our gratitude and make us indebted to him? Did he only want to show off? Maybe he had to hide stolen goods among people without attracting attention? In any case, such a sudden intrusion on our privacy was outrageous.

Some speakers pointed out that these were exactly the days, with asylum issues and demonstrations everywhere, when even the most level-headed men can go off the rails. Some excused him as a victim of societal change, others speculated about a whiplash injury. A third group's guess was an alcohol or drug problem. Only Lisa Weber, that naive chick, thought Gantenbein was „terribly nice".

After some toing and froing, Fridolin Blumer, the graveyard manager, suggested to inquire at the town council whether Gantenbein had a criminal record or perhaps a mental illness. In addition, he offered to contact his friend at the bank robbery department of the police station.

The two days that Blumer spent on background checks were rather embarrassing, since nobody knew what should be the right attitude towards Gantenbein. Should you say hello in a friendly way or maybe even, God forbid, cheerily thank him? Or perhaps better to discreetly avoid him? When he drove through our street every morning and evening, everybody disappeared from the scene just to be on safe side. In the end, on the 24th of December, came the confirmation: nothing, nothing in the least could be found on Walter Gantenbein. He was 59, divorced, no children and worked at an insurance company. The only evidence of an abnormal transaction was registered at the town council on the 7th of June 2015, stating that a certain G. had spent 10,000 francs with the aim of "bringing joy to people". Blumer proposed that everyone should now decide for themselves how to proceed with the matter.

Taking in this message we sat down together with the Pfisters and Nussbaumers and discussed our next steps. After three cups of coffee with "Pflümli" liqueur we reached the unanimous decision to keep the gift, express modest thanks and be vigilant in the future.

***

Ever since we have been looking forward to the Advent season with caution and suspicion, anticipating another present from the end of the street. Gantenbein, whom we meanwhile started to call fondly GB or Goldbein, has not attracted attention with his further extravagance, except he has grown a beard and as of the last year is disseminating the pieces of gold in person. Besides, according to a well-informed source, he has a red coat hanging in his wardrobe.

Whether there is any truth in rumours that he has obtained a small donkey for this year, will be seen in the coming days.

Homemade truffles

The very first time is crystal clear in my memory. These dark, rich truffle balls, laying next to each other on the pale-pink silk paper, luxurious and tempting, aside a fir sprig: the famous truffles of my Auntie Olga. I had just had my twenty-fifth birthday, moved out and started a promising job in the bank. Obviously, I must have done something right. Receiving Auntie Olga's truffles, you know, did not only indicate the forthcoming Christmas but it was a personal reward. Whoever got these could consider themselves to „belong" and become a fully-fledged member of society. Our beloved auntie only gave her confectionary creations to people of long-standing and solid repute. Preconditions for acceptance to the circle of the chosen ones included a respectable lifestyle, impeccable manners and a decent job in general, as well as expert knowledge in the art of cookery in particular. Someone like my cousin Franz, for example, did not stand the slightest chance. As a local butcher, he could never have reached the stage of understanding the nuanced subtleties of the cocoa-powdered coating and the gooey, bittersweet centre. Another one waiting in vain for years for a tribute from Auntie Olga, was Ida, the little poor thing. However, after her liaison with one Spaniard (and an ordinary builder at that) had become known, she was officially notified that she need not wait any longer. It did not go much better for Marianne about whom there were rumours she had joined the Greens. They say that she was honoured with the sweets from Olga only once.

***

One can naturally understand that my well-meaning auntie did not want to waste her creations on simpletons. The recipe was a well-kept secret after all, in the family for generations, always passed on from mother to daughter. Even so, it was not difficult to guess it included hazelnuts, cream, sugar and chocolate. What nobody ever found out were the proportions, temperatures and equipment that had been used. My sister Anna once thought she had uncovered the secret, but she could only produce some lumpy blobs. My auntie just gave a pitiful smile and crossed poor Anna off her list.

***

At first, in the days before Christmas, we used to leave the precious gift casually on the side table so that any guests would know immediately who they were dealing with. In hindsight, I admit it was possibly a bit unfair towards Franz, my cousin. The extent of his suffering was evident in his miserable attempt to fight back with homemade sausages. However, sausages as Christmas tree decorations did not really catch on in our family. Not least because of the four-legged pets who got mischievously excited.

Other family members who had been shamefully ignored also had a tough time accepting their fate. Ida even broke up with her Spaniard only to fall into the arms of a Portuguese shortly afterwards, who however, had the advantage of being a cook himself and making sweets of his own. Anna made efforts to break into the circle, enrolling in a computer course, joining a literature club, taking karate lessons and cleaning our auntie's windows once a week. Bitchy gossips saw all this as an attempt aimed solely at getting hold of the recipe. And Marianne – hardened by street demonstrations – created a proper family row when she trampled all over the precious truffles on our light-beige Berber rug and screamed hysterically that she had had enough of this idiotic hoo-hah, which had nothing whatsoever to do with Christmas. We never saw her again. She must have got fully immersed in dirty party politics.

***

The years passed, Christmases came and went, the truffles arrived, got ceremoniously displayed and more or less ceremoniously eaten. Unfortunately, the number of pre-Christmas guests shrank every year. Shortly after the disappearance of Marianne, cousin Franz left. He emigrated to Australia where he was reported to have had great success producing Swiss sausages. Anna made herself scarce several weeks before Christmas. Judging by the smell that came out of her kitchen window, she must have been busy with some sweets. Ida however, had met a Turkish confectioner.

***

Our dear auntie was not bothered by these events. In the meantime, I had celebrated my fortieth birthday and I was still on her list. Once we forgot the truffles on the windowsill where we had placed them while cleaning the side table. Since the radiator was exactly under that windowsill, by the end of February the truffles were not far from looking like old, wrinkled walnuts. Another time, a fresh June morning, I caught our tomcat Jimmy playing with a black truffle ball under the sofa…

To be honest, I never liked chocolate in the first place. The stuff melts all over your tongue and sticks unpleasantly to the teeth. As we know, dental treatment is not exactly cheap. What's more, time has not passed without leaving a trace on my waistline. I mainly allow myself rice wafers for breakfast. What sense would it make eating truffles after that? Fortunately, as time went by, we discovered that actually we did not really have to eat Olga's creations. They offered a cheerful decoration when air-dried and sprayed with neon colours.

***

Of-course, we could not disappoint our dear auntie. Just a mild casual remark that maybe this time something different…? Still, be it a postcard from a wellness resort or enthusiastic talk about our most recent diet – nothing brought about the desired goal. Not even escaping into the mountains helped; Olga tracked down the address. Last year we tried to cajole her with phrases like „it is too much for you...". Auntie Olga just smiled unyieldingly. Two weeks before Christmas they were there again, like always: dark, rich balls, disgustingly sweet, sticky and calorific. We were rescued by Bello, the lovely shepherd dog of the neighbour.

***

Just between you and me: it cannot continue like this! I am getting a rash just at the thought of the truffles. Something must change!

***

By the way, the postman just rang the doorbell and left a parcel at the door.

A change indeed: Olga has struck again.

A Splendid Christmas

This Christmas, our family had been exemplary. Wish lists were already prepared in September pointing out not only how the item should look, but also giving recommendations for the date and place of purchase. Uncle Ernst had taken care of reserving a laptop case; Auntie Mathilde enclosed with the wish list a completed order form for the favoured department store and my sister Monika kindly offered to buy the cashmere jumper herself. My hubby had brought home race-skis from a summer sale already in August and the little darlings made everything even easier: all they wanted was money.

With this, all preconditions for an efficient Christmas were met. My own present had also been arranged. I had personally tasked the secretary of my husband to send the invoice to him for a necklace I had bought online.

***

Therefore, Christmas passed without interrupting the work or social life – a proof of good planning.

The otherwise challenging job of guessing the needs and wishes of dear relatives was completely absent. I kept calm at the sight of glistening Christmas decorations in the streets which normally plagued me with a bad conscience every year. Christmas tree baubles and fir sprigs in shop windows failed to speed up my heartbeat; I was not shaken even at nerve-racking warnings like „Christmas in three weeks" or „Parcels can be sent until the 17th of December". While my neighbours baked the obligatory Christmas cookies, braving the oven heat and cinnamon smell, and my friends rushed from one shop to the other and soothed their sore feet in camomile tea, I was sprawling on a comfy armchair enjoying South Pacific holiday catalogues or spending time on lavish beauty care.

***

I felt most sorry for the kids who, just barely free from the school stress, had to braid coasters and decorate napkins every evening as well as Sundays under the watchful eye of their mothers, only to be followed by reciting poems or practicing little ditties. I mused smugly about our children who had uploaded their flute sonatinas during the summer holidays. They were now free from the daunting Christmas preparations and could enjoy the first snow. It goes without saying that Christmas Eve itself was also meticulously pre-planned to ensure an environmental-friendly and smooth execution. Accordingly, instead of the endlessly boring Advent wreaths, our daughter had prepared several vegan artworks using deep-fried vegetables. Not only did it look good, but it was edible as well.

***

Christmas Eve began as pleasantly as the Advent. At 19:00, the family gathered in the dining room – ladies in floor-length dresses, men in black tie, kids in „Gucci for Girls" and the tablecloth by Versace – for drinks and snacks. At 19:15, Uncle Ernst gave thanks for the invitation in well-chosen words; 19:30, the stuffed turkey was served with vegetable sides and from 19:40 until 20:55 everybody was sitting at the table. At exactly 21:00, as had been planned, the doors to the living room opened offering a magnificent view to the festively glowing Christmas tree. From this distance nobody realised that it was in fact, a digital hologram that could easily be projected anywhere – 2 meters wide and 2.30 high, 55 candles, 55 baubles and two 5-meter lengths of tinsel – changing colour every 15 minutes. It ran either in a standard mode – red, violet, gold, dark blue, silver – or it could be manually programmed.

It was a unique designer item with seasonal options that could be used all year round on different settings. For example, from June to September „Coconut palm trees on a sandy beach" or in October „Deer in autumn colours".

I have to say it was a touching moment! The flute recordings by our children provided pleasant background music and we entered the living room that had been decorated with a lot of care by a well-known event organiser. They had thought about everything: presents were neatly stacked next to the tree. There were enough scissors and bins to assist speedy and tidy unwrapping.

And then it happened: the family of my brother forced their way into our house in their notorious noisy and clumsy way, taking no notice of the celebration hour. (I must add here that my brother had not been welcome in the family for quite some time – his standing was not quite on par with ours). So, this brother of mine, his wife and the mob of kids spread out shamelessly in our living room, under our tree and next to our presents. That could have been tolerable perhaps, since one must not hold a grudge against someone, even if he is the black sheep, when he wants to return to the safety of family on Christmas Eve. However, we were all shocked at the audacity when he started distributing presents – presents that nobody had either ordered or chosen and that were just imposed on us! I could not believe my eyes when I was suddenly holding a braided coaster and I saw Auntie Mathilde unfolding a decorated napkin.

But that was not all. When my auntie saw the horrible, tasteless napkins, she actually started to rub her eyes and mumble words like „oh, how lovely". My sister Monika even got carried away with a thank-you kiss, just because she received a set of self-knitted, greyish-white potholders from the messy urchins of my brother. Indeed, even my Uncle Ernst, who is a deputy director at an investment bank and as such very much known as a pragmatist, snivelled audibly.

***

What should I say! The evening did not go as planned. Everything that had been carefully prepared was destroyed in one fell swoop. As it happened, despite all the goodwill, our family still failed to have the perfect Christmas Eve…

The Gift Expert

Already from birth, my Uncle Alfred was a special person. Not only was he bigger and heavier than other toddlers, oh no. His intelligence and willpower was also outstanding even in the cradle. As young as ten days old he was energetically snatching the milk bottle and at three-months old, he made his first successful attempt at standing up. He set tongues wagging in the kindergarten when he auctioned all his toys in order to buy shares. By the age of twenty-five, he had two doctoral degrees and owned a yacht in the Mediterranean sea.

Hence, the day he established his own company was no big surprise to anyone. Of-course it wasn't just any old company. Even though he could have done anything, he didn't become a business consultant, software developer or leasing agent. The mission he took on could be best described as „commercial altruism". That is to say, he succeeded in filling one of the biggest market gaps and at the same time resolving a burning social issue: he became a gift expert.

He was acutely shrewd in recognising the nationwide market opportunities available from annual gift giving. He undertook serious calculations and demonstrated that just in Switzerland alone the same amount of hours is spent thinking about what gift to give to who as it is spent on the production of 500 million quality watches. If one were to include also the time spent choosing the presents, standing in queues at cash desks, dealing with wrong deliveries and returns, the numbers would amount to three times the export volume of Switzerland. However, as my Uncle Alfred pointed out in his new book, one must factor in not only the direct time spent but also the indirect productivity loss caused by the disappointments and frustrations around receiving and giving gifts. Any half-wit can easily imagine the huge opportunities for economic growth if gift-giving would be concentrated to a few hubs or persons. Taking this into account, it would not be an exaggeration to describe the business of my uncle as a disruptive innovation.

***

Success set in without delay. The early clients were mainly transportation companies, banks and architects' offices, but as time went by ever more private individuals joined as well. Everyone, from young entrepreneurs to wealthy patrons, was soon turning to Alfred. So it came that after a few years the startup was turning over money that one should only whisper about.

In the beginning, he dealt with each case in person, undertook intensive character studies and stepped into the shoes of the person giving the gift or the person receiving it, or both. That reflected his deep dedication which made him engage also with the emotional side of gift-giving. The main thing, as he disclosed to me once, is about bringing joy: „Someone must do it in the end."

His empathy was bordering on selflessness. I saw him on the verge of an identity crisis many times. When he was prancing down the street from the train station, I knew that he was dealing with an order from an orchestra conductor. Another time, seeing him navigate the traffic with a furrowed brow and a flickering gaze, he undoubtedly must have been tasked by a stockbroker.

However, these days were soon over. The ever-growing demand forced him to install computers and, not long afterwards, double their processing power several times. He soon owned an elaborate data management system, keeping track of the newest products all over the world and comparing these with the wishes of clients. In case of a match, the system independently raised an order, drafted suitable greeting cards and issued invoices. All my Uncle Alfred had to do, was to upload the client's data, the rest was handled by the computer system.

Alfred would not have been himself had he not launched yet another product line for his own range of unique gift proposals and creations. Furthermore, he even launched an annual special edition that became a must-have for anyone wishing to „belong". Rumour has it that some people bought those just only not be left out from small talk. In short: Alfred became an international cult figure offering high society a truly merry and carefree Christmas.

No wonder that many competitors tried shamelessly to copy his ideas, albeit without success. Alfred was always a step ahead and nobody could even get close to his mastery. For example, he was the first one to launch a VirtualReality-Xmas-App in corona times for cosy virus-free singles evenings. This proved to be a ground-breaking hit. Initially the app came as part of a set which included a CD with five different Christmas themes, each appealing to a particular taste or imagination. The set also included theme-matching room fragrance and a music list with 560 songs by top artists as well as the option of foie gras, pre-cooked turkey leg, a drink selection (Champagne, white wine or red wine) and/or half a dozen delightfully decorated microwaved cupcakes. It barely took a week until a further package of individual Christmas tree designs was available, which allowed buyers to redecorate their trees directly on the screen during Christmas Eve. For the next year, it was already announced that the optional design would include virtual guests.

It goes without saying that our family, to be precise the entire clan, also relied on Uncle Alfred and I can confirm that we were never disappointed. Be it birthdays, weddings or Christmas, his deliveries were always on time, tasteful and well-priced. Since we all knew each other and everyone was familiar with the gift arrangements, we did not keep secrets and notified each other of our wishes via Internet. Doing so, the thank-you cards could be printed at the same time as the congratulation cards, offering an irresistible discount. The gift-givers only had to check the balance on their bank accounts once a year since their dues were deducted automatically. Compared with earlier times, our family saved a massive amount of time and we toyed with the idea to leave out compliment slips or thank-you cards in order to increase productivity. However, things did not turn out as planned.

***

Even today, I am still profoundly shocked that, of all times, it had to happen at Christmas. First we thought that our dear uncle might be dealing with a personal crisis, triggered by a sudden illness or a burnout. Then we suspected a labour dispute in the computer network industry, which – as we all know – can develop their own unpredictable dynamics. Finally, we dreaded blackmail by cyber criminals. Or maybe it was an algorithm running wild?

Without delay, the family engaged a well-known security firm to investigate whether there had been interference from hostile elements, power-hungry software giants or envious startups.

It was soon clear, however, that none of that was true. The catastrophe was triggered by Alfred himself, in full command of mind and body. A sad sign that even geniuses make mistakes. The incident was blown wide open on the 14th December, just at the peak of the high season. This is the date when the flowers were due to arrive for my mother-in-law's birthday. Nothing came. Alfred's phone lines were dead.

Of course, it did not take long until worried clients called the telecom helpline and, in despair, they alerted the police.

In the meantime, quite many people had clicked on Alfred's homepage, causing it to crash within half an hour. There was nothing but a plain message: „ Sorry - this site is no longer available".

It didn't make any sense: at the time when hundreds of thousands, if not millions, had put their hopes on Alfred, he had shamefully turned his back on them. The moment of panic and bewilderment was followed by anger. More than a hundred customers rushed to the headquarters where they combined forces and smashed down the door. Some were still hoping that not everything was lost – perhaps you just had to push the button and the gift carousel would be up and running again. This hope did not last long. True to his nature, Alfred had taken care of everything. Customer data were deleted and all screens gleefully flickered „Merry Christmas".

The damage was immeasurable. One day has never seen so many nervous breakdowns and hysterics. It was the 14th of December and there were no presents! Christmas was seriously in danger.

It is appalling to think back how helpless and defeated we were, confronted again with the insurmountable problems of the forthcoming celebration. In one go we were back to what we believed was gone for good: exhausting rumination, time-consuming search for presents, queueing at cash desks, wrong deliveries and returns. Oh Alfred, what have you done to mankind!

It was much later that we learnt what had happened. In the evening of the 13th of December, shortly before 8pm, Alfred had been in his office alone installing additional hard drives to accommodate the booming Christmas business when someone must have called on him. Not suspecting any harm, he rushed to open the door, probably thinking there was an urgent gift request. However, instead of a client a bizarre, otherworldly creature stood at the door holding a candle. Without any warning, the creature – blond and female, according to the reports – handed him a parcel wrapped in silk paper labelled „Present".

Just imagine, he - the biggest gift-giver in the world – just received a present. That must have blown his mind. You cannot explain his reaction in any other way. He told us that he took the box (by the way, it simply contained a mirror) and knew immediately that he must bring about a radical change. The very same evening, prompted by an inner voice, he deleted all programs irreversibly. No more heartless nonsense!

Alfred has never been the same since. His cool and calculating mind, his talent for innovation, his luck in investments – in short, everything that we admired – had given way to suspiciously high spirits and a laid-back attitude, nearly like that of a light-headed child. He has retreated to a desolate place in the South – I would rather not tell you the name for security reasons – and he takes care of dozens of olive trees as well as three goats. He sends me a basket full of figs every year.

We, however, have been wracking our brains about Christmas presents. The macroeconomic consequences are disastrous.

The Master Chef

He was the one you would call a master of his profession. Drawing upon the unique combination of outstanding technical skills, surprising imagination, stylish judgment and a fervent drive to improve, he had worked his way up from a dishwasher in a mediocre hotel to an extraordinary top chef and a connoisseur of good food. His signature dishes were famous at home and abroad, his recipes quietly spread from one kitchen to the next. The gourmet popes showered him with stars and hat awards. „A fusion-kitchen combining fascinating exotics, French charm and Alpine tradition", cheered one of them. „A visionary mix of genius molecular cookery with macrobiotic highlights", raved another.

Every evening the so-called elite society begged for a table reservation – if need be, on knees – since anyone who wanted to be anyone must have had tried the „Mousse au Cognac" at least once. His "Allgäu wild boar carpaccio" was equally legendary, served with Pacific seaweed draped over ice from a Swiss glacier, and an entrecôte nestled in deep-fried hay. The latter was so delicate and aromatic because it had been ridden soft under a horse saddle in Appenzellerland for 48 hours as is the ancient Hun tradition. Farmhouse ham, matured one week in the smoke of barbecued car tyres and described as an „aromatic hocus-pocus" by one gastro-journal, was another guarantee of global attention, even if it was not to everyone's taste. However, the topic created predictably heated discussion between dinner courses or, so to speak, an Amuse-Bouche.

Therefore it was certainly not a big surprise that the „Grand Dîner Surprise de Noël" was booked out already a year ahead. The privileged clients knew that the evening would become the new high point.

Indeed, this year the chef had come up with something very special: the Haute-Couture Menu including the most exquisite ingredients from across the world that would be part of live plating shows at the table. Accordingly, the preparations had been running at full speed for months. The menu, consisting of 24 courses, was set out already in the summer. The chef himself had started the sublime herbal liqueur which would refine the sauce for the main course - „Suprême de faisan aux écrevisse sauté et bonbon de pêche". He had also ordered the langoustines, vital for the sole rolls with lobster sauce, since these had to crawl around in aroma-infused seawater for at least two months.

Everything ran like clockwork during the rehearsal dinner on the 17th of December. The wine temperature was ideal, champagne corks popped at the right time, the duck liver terrine melted in the mouth. Bizarrely however, the Christmas vibe was missing. It could not have been the fault of the food. Neither could it have been because of the decorations. A well-known interior design company had delivered candles, artificial fir sprigs and baubles, rolled out a midnight blue carpet with golden stars in front of the entrance and had installed an antique Baroque angel (carved lindenwood, Southern Germany, 18th century) over the kitchen door.

Suddenly it clicked. The chef's intuition told him what was missing from the perfect Christmas experience: the snow!

***

As had become the norm for quite some years already, not a single snowflake had fallen in the lowlands of the central region. The sky was bright blue and the weather forecast for the coming weeks did not give any hope for clouds.

No time to lose. When the sky is not up to the duty, technology must help out. Fortunately, one is no longer dependent on the whims of the weather. Snowmaking can easily be done by machines – what's right for ski resorts, is also fair enough for a master chef.

The required snow guns were rushed in as well as water pipes and electric power lines. On the 24th of December, at exactly eight o'clock in the morning, the snow was blasted out from three-jet cannons. What a marvellous sight!

Indoors, the napkins were folded into elf hats and a cinnamon glaze was spooned over "Petit fours aux noix".

Outside, a soft white blanket of snow fell on grass, bushes and trees.

Five o'clock in the evening, the garden was covered with thick snow. The chef looked approvingly out of the window and ordered the snow operation to stop. He then put on a fresh chef's hat, washed his hands ceremoniously and moved to put the final touches on his culinary creations.

However, man proposes, God disposes.

Looking out of the window again at six o'clock, he noticed to his annoyance that his order had been ignored. It was still snowing. Since he was busy folding the egg whites into the artichoke purée, he had to suppress his anger and let his sous-saucier go to check the situation.

He could barely start on his truffles in blankets, when the Maître de Service rushed into the kitchen. He was paler than his white tuxedo and asked to have a word with the boss. While he was fully aware that peace and concentration is essential for a chef, he felt compelled to pass on important information: it looked as though a catastrophe was looming. For an hour and a half, they had tried to stop the snow machine. Without success. The entire control panel as well as the taps were covered with a thick layer of ice and it was impossible to turn off the water or power supply. All the tinkering had been in vain - the snow was out of control. There was nothing to be seen of the blue carpet.

***

The chef abandoned his pots and rushed, cursing and swearing, from the kitchen to the dining room and back. Losing his temper did not help. Specialists from „Speedy Plumbers" were called in, but they were as useless as the fire brigade whose truck got stuck already on the way. It snowed on and on and on.

The white wonder was piling up at the windows at an unbelievable speed. Already some time ago, the parking area and garden had completely disappeared. The chef held his head in his hands and was about to accept his fate when he heard a faint snap. He looked up and saw that the Baroque angel had pulled a wry face. Was it possible that … could it be … ?

„What should I do?" whimpered the chef. „I am ready to sacrifice everything, please help me out of this disaster."

„Everything won't be necessary," whispered the angel. „I am happy with just fifty percent of the turnover."

The chef's heart nearly stopped. „Fifty percent?" he gasped, „What do you need it for?"

The angel winked and stretched out an arm towards the village church.

„For that?", asked the chef.

And the angel nodded and smiled.

Then there was a spooky change, later described by all the witnesses as a miracle.

The chef was still standing by the kitchen door when it started to rain - big, heavy raindrops fell, first slowly and then ever heavier until a torrential downpour washed over the area. Almost at the same time, the out-of-control snow machines turned into water cannons. The ice was melting and the snow clumped up. It didn't even take an hour until the pesky snow had pretty much disappeared. At the drive-in, a snowman suddenly popped out of nowhere holding an arrow sign, unmistakably pointing in the direction of the church. Arriving guests followed the sign in high spirits, all the more so as the bells began chiming. Clearly, it was part of the programme! Such an

original idea! A real „Surprise de Noël" or, as one lady put it: „a truly heavenly surprise".
Everybody agreed that this festive introduction was another high of the chef's legendary sense of style.

By now, of course, all the candles, baubles and fir sprigs along with the midnight blue carpet have been cleared out. Only the angel is hanging over the kitchen door and pointing with an outstretched arm to the church opposite. It is not known whether there were more negotiations between the angel and the chef. The church, in any case, could afford new chairs and quotes were recently taken for the facade renovation. There are rumours that a donor who prefers anonymity was regularly making larger contributions.

Well, those who can put two and two together and observe the ever-increasing price of the „Mousse au Cognac", may expect a new church organ in the near future.

A Little Bit of Time

Every year before Christmas, preferably during the grey foggy days of November, a delegation of angels is sent to the world with the assignment to find out how to bring joy to people. The big angels fly to big cities and the small angels fly to small towns – all according to the everlasting heavenly rules of procedure.

When the envoys return a week later, a big celebratory conference is convened where all proposals are assessed, decisions are taken and duties allocated. The surprises are delivered discreetly around Christmas, so that everything looks like a coincidence, but still visible enough to everyone. It is just that these days people do not believe in miracles anymore and quite a few of the gifts from above go unnoticed.

***

This year was no exception. Exactly on the first of December, the host of angels met for the festive conference – the big ones above and the small ones underneath, according to the letter of the heaven rules.

„Dear ladies and gentlemen," said the archangel who was chairing the meeting, „let us thinketh and consulteth each other on what will bring joy to people. Every one of us should speak up."

The words of the archangel faded away under the dome of the endless heavenly universe and silence set in among the angels. Minutes passed and no one was making any proposals. Finally, one of the oldest angels raised a hand and said: „Peace, shouldn't we bring peace to all people? This has always been our task."

The entire host of angels chanted in unison: „Peace". Then, however, the archangel shook his head: „We have been bringing peace for 2000 years and without any success. It's time to think of something new."

„Money," a voice from the middle of the table called out, „that is what people desire most."

The archangel shook his head again: „My dear friends, we cannot bring money. That is the business of our competitors from below."

„Health", offered an old, pensive angel. „Health is so very important to people. They spend a lot of time and money on it."

But again, the archangel shook his head: „As far as the health branch is concerned, people only believe in their own concoctions. We do not stand a chance against the chemical industry."

„How about love?", asked a meddlesome little angel whose rosy, chubby cheeks were suspiciously similar to those of Cupid.

And again, the archangel shook his head: „We tried love last year. The consequences were devastating." (He turned red in the face). „Apparently the people got our message wrong."

***

What to do? It became compellingly clear that being an angel was getting trickier with time.

Silence fell again over the host of angels.

Suddenly there was a hushed voice from under the table.

„Time," whispered a little angel, who then fell silent with embarrassment.

However, the archangel nodded cheerfully: „True, little angel, you are right. Lack of time is people's biggest disease, even if it is a disease that they themselves bring upon themselves."

Then a hustle and bustle started. The concept was elaborated, an agenda put together, costs calculated and facilitating measures launched.

***

So it happened that on the 20th of December, strange things started to come about. Big cities and small towns were plagued with blackouts. Suddenly, here and there the lights went off. In a certain city with a river and many beautiful shops, it happened on the 22nd of December at 6pm on the dot. Trams came to a standstill, traffic lights switched off, cash registers jammed, radios and TVs fell silent, PCs, washing machines, electric mixers and shaving machines suddenly stopped.

***

Mrs Stoll was just standing in the kitchen when she noticed to her horror that the ceiling light as well as the oven lamp went off and the roast stopped sizzling. All that exactly at the time when her husband was at the door receiving guests.

Two houses down, the family Nagel were having cheese sandwiches and watching a TV quiz. Just when the contestant was about to reply to the tie-break question, the image started flickering and disappeared as a ghost. The only audible sound was „aarrgghh..".

Mrs Niedermann was hit even worse. She got stuck in the elevator at the shopping centre with her haughty neighbours, carrying a forty-franc ice cream cake.

The case of Director Haubensack was tragic since he was on his way to a crucial meeting concerning Swiss foreign trade and he was locked between the first and the second panels of the revolving door of his office building.

An extraordinary session of the city council, the staff Christmas dinner at the hospital, the vernissage event of the art club, a concert in the community centre, the Christmas market in the central square, shopping, hustle and bustle, hooting and hollering, tugging and nudging – all stopped dead.

***

Darkness spread over the city. Not so much a cold, frightening darkness, but rather a big warm blanket that wrapped you in comfort. A thousand stars glistened and sparkled above like a crown of a huge Christmas tree.

One after each other, lights lit up on earth as well. Here in a window, there on a table, even in the streets, buses and trains – little Christmas candles were lit everywhere, and the ocean of flickering lights competed with the ones over the horizon.

***

Mrs Stoll did not need to worry. The guests were really thrilled with the emergency solution of sausages and bread. They were so pleased that later in the evening they decided to organise such unconventional gatherings more often in the future.

The Nagels didn't even notice how they ended up in the middle of a lively debate – for the first time in two years – and the father discovered to his surprise that the boys had actually quite reasonable views.

Mrs Niedermann was also surprised: she had to recognise, despite her conviction, that the new neighbours were actually not as bad as she had thought. When she was offered an apple, she unpacked the ice cream cake which had started to melt. What is the problem if there is only cold orange juice available instead of hot coffee: there will be another coffee meet-up soon anyway.

Director Haubensack did not have it so comfortable. He still managed to sit down. Since he could not do anything else, he decided to call his daughter who lived in America. He had a photo of her together with her child in his briefcase. He knelt down, created a flame with his cigarette lighter and looked at the photo. A warm feeling came to his heart hearing her voice so clear and near.

***

After two hours, the lights were back on, machines started humming, trams continued their journeys, automatic doors re-opened and it looked on the surface as if everything was back to normal. Some were cursing about the mishap, some were laughing. But here and there, slight changes had occurred. Barely visible and by no means sensational. The next day, there was a short notice in the newspaper stating there had been a power outage in the city the day before.

Well, people do not believe in miracles these days. Even the most precious gifts from above go unnoticed most of the time. It is a pity, because you never know what might come around the next time! Think about it when the lights go off, traffic gets stuck in snow or when there is freezing rain: maybe, just maybe, there is an angel at work trying to give people a little bit of time. And not only at Christmas time...

The Annoying Experience of Mrs B

I admit it now – I fibbed sometimes in my earlier Christmas stories. Now however, the time has come to talk about an actual event. It unfolded not far from here, in a tax efficient location near a lake, beginning with the letter K. The central character was a certain Mrs B – a busy wife of a well-known real estate agent, daughter of a wealthy industrialist, chic, charming, active and the centre of attention at countless cocktail parties.

***

It all started on the 18th of December, when Mrs B had one spare hour between the deli and the hairdresser which could be used for thinking about Christmas. She sat down on the blue sofa in her blue lounge and flicked through the brochures and catalogues that had piled up in the house during recent days and weeks.

What present should she give to her husband this time? He already had a golden cigarette lighter, crocodile leather briefcase and precious stone cufflinks. Last year, she had bought him a sterling silver stationery set. The latest gadget he would normally buy for himself and wine was brought annually by his colleagues. What else was out there?

A platinum napkin ring made no sense since they ate at home very rarely. He was still too young for a duck head handle walking cane and a shaving mirror on a marble stand would be too old-fashioned. 40 minutes and 13 catalogues later she concluded with irritation that Christmas promoters had not given her a single good idea. What would have been the point of a vegan phone case or a mini-Buddha including a meditation manual?

Then she noticed a flyer that was stuck in between the catalogues. „An ideal present for all! NOTHING brings more joy!" was written in big bold letters. Intrigued, she continued reading: „Let our Christmas service surprise you. Top package offer: a tree, jewellery, presents and stylish presentation based on Angel&Co designs in gold, silver and pink. Prompt service, discreet delivery. One call is enough."

That was exactly what she was after. A trustworthy company who would take on the entire burden of thinking and buying. That would save time and be original on top. She quickly took out the phone and ordered the luxury edition in gold. Everything was done in three minutes.

***

The days until the 24th flew by with vernissages, concerts, premieres and dinners. Mrs B had hardly any time left for the beauty parlour, sauna and solarium.

Suitably styled and curled, Mrs B sat with her husband in the blue lounge. Exactly at the agreed time the door opened. Two charming golden blonde creatures wafted into the room carrying an exquisite gold spray-painted Christmas tree – decorated with golden angels and golden candles – and a dozen glittering packages. It was an exemplary service. The creatures laid the delivery on the blue carpet in front of the blue sofa, lit the candles and disappeared as smoothly as they had arrived. A really discreet business.

„Congratulations", said Mr B approvingly to his wife. „Once again you managed to hit the nail on the head."

For four minutes they admired the tree and then turned to open the packages. After all, they did not have too much time as they were also on the guest list for the customary Christmas party hosted by the bank governor.

However, already the first package perplexed Mrs B. She did not have anything but an empty box in front of her. Apparently, someone had forgotten to put something in there. A logistics mistake, perhaps. She would ask for a refund of at least 10% off the bill.

She quickly moved to the next package. To her horror, this was also empty. Was this possibly done on purpose? Was someone pulling her leg? Hands shaking, she went on to the next package: nothing. Suddenly she twigged, recalling the bold print on the flyer: „NOTHING brings more joy".

The face of her husband confirmed the scandal. He looked sheepishly at the crinkled papers in his hands. NOTHING. She had really given him NOTHING for

Christmas. In this tense moment something wonderful happened. The little golden angels on the Christmas tree started to smile and sing with celestial voices. The blue lounge was suddenly filled with peace and joy, bringing both Bs to a hearty laugh. The anger turned into happiness and annoyance into harmony. With relief, they looked at the golden candles, even brighter now than earlier and forgot completely that they had to go to the party.

For the first time, it became Christmassy in the blue lounge.

***

This was the story about family B in city K. Or at least, it could have been like this. This overwhelming Christmas spirit is making me fib again. Of course, it was completely different. No joy and harmony whatsoever! Mr B played nervously with his silk tie and Mrs B slammed her diamond-decorated hand down on the blue couch. „Not with me," she screamed loud in the blue lounge. „I want to have my presents now!". They dialled the number of Angel&Co in fury.

There however, was only a recorded message „Merry and Peaceful Christmas", followed by a strange celestial music.

I better not repeat here what Mrs B said, or rather screamed and how Mr B reacted. I just have to add that all phone calls and written complaints, including the one from the family attorney, brought no success. The company Angel&Co had disappeared into NOTHING. No wonder!

The Flight to Mombasa

Perhaps you can still recall this: Exactly two years ago, on the 25th of December, an Airbus A330 owned by TransitAir went missing flying over the Libyan desert. The plane had started out from Zurich airport at 18.10 local time with 298 passengers and 12 crew members on board. Eight and a half hours later it was meant to have landed in Mombasa. Between 21:00 and 22:00 the traffic control tower in Tripoli received suspicious signals that were later interpreted as calls for help. However, the radio messaging did not follow. The plane went missing for about seven hours until it suddenly appeared again in the morning of the 26th of December in Zurich.

***

The episode hardly made it to the news since nobody was injured. Just only one tabloid wrote about the mysterious event while the mainstream press took it as fake news and ignored it. Yet, the paper had a point. Something bizarre did happen during that night. I can affirm it because I am fully aware of the details. As it happens, my Uncle Julius and my Aunt Lisette were among the passengers. Exhausted by the annual winter sports frenzy, they had decided to take a two-week beach holiday at the Kenyan seaside – a „rendez-vous with the sun" according to the travel brochure – not least in order to rejuvenate their complexions for the forthcoming automobile club ball.

At the start, everything went smoothly. The aircraft looked like all aircrafts of this type always do. There was nothing extraordinary about the airport procedures either. The check-in time was a bit longer than usual, but this was solely because of one annoying person wanting to check in seventeen pieces of luggage. The flight attendants smiled in their normal way if not even a tad friendlier. According to my uncle, one of them was especially attractive – bright blue eyes, long shiny blond hair, graceful and charming. In short, almost an angel.

The take-off was exactly on schedule. Everybody leant back and relaxed. Only the Bern chaps in seats No 26c and 26d could not contain their excitement. Anyway, their „Woo-hoos" were drowned out by the roaring of the engines. One family with two kids stood out with their repeated „psst". All the other passengers behaved like regular flyers. One was looking for interesting tax-free items in the on-board magazine. Another concentrated on the economics column of the Neue Zürcher Zeitung. There was a bored girl flipping through fashion magazines.

Dinner was served at 19:00 CET and the menu reflected the festive evening in its opulence. Sparkling wine with salted peanuts were served as the appetizer, followed by chicken liver pâté and olives, a small salad bouquet and smoked trout with lingonberry and horseradish foam. Then filet steak with rice and tomatoes, a piece of gâteau and a cheese selection. Loudspeakers were playing gentle Christmas carols. The captain wished Merry Christmas in three languages and pointed out that they were flying over the Mediterranean. The stewardesses walked from one passenger to the other shaking hands. My uncle commented that the brief contact with the blond angel had left a lasting impression. Something about this woman was different than the others, somehow more personal and welcoming. It also looked as if she was drifting past the rows of seats, instead of walking. In the dim light you might even have thought there were two little wings on her back, which was clearly nonsense.

***

The dinner service carried on for a while. Some people were becoming affected by the sparkling wine. Two fat ones sitting near the emergency exit were roaring with laughter, one baldie used the opportunity to pat a stewardess secretly, a bearded one in jeans and an unbuttoned shirt entertained his row with tales of his African experiences.

Mystical events started to unfold when the coffee was being served. A hefty Father Christmas figure with a huge cap, in a gold embroidered coat and never-ending beard suddenly appeared in the middle of the cabin as if by magic. Everyone clapped their hands happily. The angelic blondie smiled in a wonderful way. Passengers did not notice that the other hostesses were somewhat at a loss, looking at each other quizzically.

Father Christmas raised his hands authoritatively and everyone fell silent. Then, with a deep voice that sounded as if coming from far away, he said loudly and solemnly „Peace on earth!" and walked off towards the cockpit in measured steps.

***

All of the passengers were excited. The airline was praised for its attention to detail in laying on the Christmas atmosphere. Many nice things were said about the dinner, which had been extraordinary for an in-flight menu. The crew were praised, especially the little blond one. In short, spirits were really high.

Therefore, nobody got worried when the plane started to sway and shake. Attention perked up only after the trays with half-finished coffee cups were whisked away and the fasten-seatbelt signs went on. What was the matter? Nobody knew. The flight attendants were pale, some of them trembling nervously. Couples clasped to each other, the Bern chaps in seats No 26c and 26d groaned „Hoo-ha" and there was a whiny „Mamma mia" in the background. There was no sight of the charming blondie.

***

Maybe after ten or fifteen minutes had passed, the plane started to gain height, ever more steeply as if it were a space rocket. It was not possible to leave the seat or even to say anything. All passengers were pressed to their chairs as if in straightjackets. The plane soared higher and higher, into the ocean of stars, more and more of which appeared by the second. Everything was glistening, shining and twinkling, turning green, then blue, then silver and gold. The light gradually took over the inside of the plane as well. At first it was weak and transparent, soon, however, it dazzled and danced over all the rows of seats, the floor, ceiling and walls wrapping everything in a blinding radiance. Next came the magical music. First it was like flutes and violins, then trumpets and kettledrums and finally something like mighty pipe-organs. It was neither ethereal music nor church music, but perhaps a mix of the two and yet still somewhat different. Then the most peculiar thing happened. The intense pressure disappeared and the passengers could move freely again. Their anxiety and fear turned into confidence and joy. Happiness spread all over and faces brightened up. As soon as one started to sing „O you joyful", everybody joined in with enthusiasm.

***

It is a bit unclear how long this exuberance lasted. What is documented is that the plane re-appeared on the radar screen in Zurich around eight o'clock in the morning and landed shortly afterwards, safe and sound. „As if out of thin air", was written in the log by the air traffic controller. It goes without saying that the police and the ambulance were immediately on the scene. However, there was not much to do. The doors of the aircraft could be opened without any problems and there was no sign of a hijacker.

Even an extended search of the plane revealed nothing. The big man in the red robe had disappeared. Just in case, the passengers and the crew were taken to hospital. Physical or psychological damage could not be found, apart from the fact that they all were humming „O you joyful" - which lasted well into January.

All the responsible authorities lost no time in searching for plausible explanations for the incident. One official communication referred to a technical malfunction of the altitude control and a lack of oxygen in the cabin that might have caused hallucinations.

Still, they were hiding one important fact. It was not only the mysterious Father Christmas who had gone missing, but also the blonde flight attendant. My uncle heard later from one of the TransitAir employees that the stewardess could not be found on the plane, and more perplexing, she did not appear on either the staff list or shift rota. Nobody had ever seen her earlier.

***

Since that event, my relatives have undergone a surprising change. They belong to an established Zurich family with traditional values and used to pay high regard to social status. But now they very often mingle with working class and undistinguished people. Once my aunt even invited the postman for a coffee. On top of that, there appeared a noticeable liking for gift-giving, which had not been in their nature earlier. Family and friends suddenly started receiving all kinds of presents. Visiting them recently, I saw a thank-you note from the Red Cross on the table. There are also rumours that my uncle had assigned a substantial amount for church renovations.

All in all, they both seem to be very happy. Their faces radiate a rare expression of satisfaction. They attract unfavourable attention only on rare occasions. Namely, when they start singing „O you joyful" on balmy summer evenings.

The Joy of Giving

Something truly bizarre happened to Charles F. Buttiker on the 23rd of December. The moment he took a break from hearings and brainstormings, marketing concepts and layout proposals and lit his 21st cigarette, he suddenly noticed a publicity campaign „The Joy of Giving" that he himself had created last spring. The sight of a super skinny girl sitting on a golden tray from the interior design company „Superior Homes" (high quality print and visually balanced graphic design) did not bring the triumphant feeling that normally kicked in when recalling a well-paid job. He was overwhelmed by a completely new sentiment that was difficult to comprehend but was really exciting. Charles F. Buttiker, the owner and director of the famous advertising agency Buttiker&Muller, was hit by a pang of desire to live up to the words printed in gold and black on the poster. He wanted to test and try out the unknown pleasure of bringing joy.

He reflected quickly whether he might not have fallen victim to his own genius. Maybe his advert was so good that it manipulated even its own creator? He examined the poster closer but far enough away for a good perspective. Doing so, he established that the shadow of the tray fell on the logo of Superior Homes giving „Superior" an ugly, subdued and lame undertone. However, even the discovery of this mistake – certainly grounds for a price reduction – did not suppress his urge to „give". Quite the opposite. It even looked to him as if the girl smiled in encouragement, which was definitely just an optical illusion.

***

The sentiment did not vanish during the following hours. Neither a double whisky nor an annoying phone call from C.P. Felsenstein concerning the „Clean laundry" assignment brought about any change. The feeling sat deeply in Charles F. Buttiker: he must do a good deed.

To be honest, the season actually favoured this kind of action. Christmas is the time for giving gifts and bringing joy after all. The problem was, however, that he had already prepared his presents – a fur coat for his wife, a cheque for his daughter, wine for the son-in-law and even a diamond for the girlfriend. Other smaller or bigger offerings were also organised for relatives and friends as well as for business contacts. What else?

Charles F. Buttiker stretched out in his director's leather chair and instructed the receptionist not to disturb him while he immersed himself in creative meditation – a talent admired, as well as dreaded, by fellow experts in advertising circles. What can one do in the 21st century in order to bring joy to people?

At first, he could only think of worn-out clichés like distributing sweets in the high street, which is something that every political party does at election time. A donation to a charity felt too impersonal while becoming a sponsor for a Third World project felt too personal. For a short time, he was toying with the idea of sending a 100 gram gold bar to all his social contacts via a courier. Then, however, he realised that in all likelihood his family would not approve. The thought of providing people with a thousand free Christmas trees, all prepared and decorated, was not that appealing either. Still, he took note of this, bearing in mind his long-standing client in furniture design.

***

One hour and fifteen more ideas later it became clear that he would never get anywhere continuing in the same way. There was an urgent need to activate method number two, which had always been most avidly envied by his competitors. It involved the so-called „Impulse-Creativity" where he had to focus on his „inner self" and let intuition flow. This secret recipe had brought Buttiker&Muller sensational success with the Export-Beer campaign in 2011.

The method drew upon the experience gathered over the past two decades, which suggested that income generating ideas are never conceived at the desk. Rather, they are triggered by certain outside influences, even if created artificially. For example, compelling slogans for foam baths, overseas travel or ice cream may be inspired by a running tap, UV lamp and Brazilian rhythms, while Beethoven and Bordeaux have proven themselves in the area of jewellery, Persian rugs and promissory notes.

***

All Charles F. Buttiker needed was a suitable influence. His office was hastily decorated with all the attributes that might be necessary for an authentic Christmas mood: smell of a roast, burnt fir sprig, artificial snow on the carpet and a photo of the Vienna Choir Boys projected on the wall.

However, as fate would happen, nothing brought about the expected effect (even though, it should be mentioned here for the sake of honesty, the same had occurred in 2005 for the ToothBlend campaign). Try as he might, the inspiration would not come.

„Earlier," he thought, „giving was much easier." In those times, there were loads of poor and humble people who would have been grateful for a sausage. But today? Where can you find today, say in Zurich, anyone who would look forward to a sausage? He felt tired, discouraged and disappointed, which was a rare occurrence in his hard but predominantly successful career. So he decided to go home.

***

It had turned dark in the meantime. The high street was glistening with Christmas lights and it was the normal five o'clock rush hour. Trams were ringing bells and creaking, brakes were squeaking, engines were booming. Joyless people with umbrellas hurried by, carrying packages, lips pursed.

In a last desperate attempt he threw a hundred note to a street musician, but the guy did not even look up. Buttiker hesitated for a moment hoping that the man's face would still brighten up in gratefulness. Nothing.

„One chance, just one is what I deserve", he thought begrudgingly as he entered the car park. His nerves were shot and his hands were trembling. He lit a cigarette to calm down – it was his forty fifth one.

And then it happened. Probably he had not switched off the lighter or he might have stepped carelessly given his frazzled state. In any case, there was a short ripping sound and the plastic bag of the lady next to him burst. All the food and household items rolled merrily out of a big round hole.

He could really do without that! He busied himself rounding up five apples, three onions, a deodorant, two boxes of paper tissues, a tin of cat food and a slightly squashed smoked salmon. Stepping back, he got ready for withering looks from the lady. However, what awaited him took his breath away. He was given a beaming, sincere, heartwarming and grateful smile. A smile that made the world lighter and brighter. Like Christmas.

„Thank you," she said softly, „many thanks for your kind help." Charles F. Buttiker did not understand what happened to him. It was exactly the feeling that he had been waiting for. What failed in creative meditation and impulse creativity was suddenly born in bumbling clumsiness. The deeper meaning and the real root of his slogan „The Joy of Giving" suddenly came home to him in all clarity.

Instinctively, he reached for his lighter, lit it and noticed that there was still enough gas.

Losing no time, he turned around, mingled with the crowds who were on their way home from work and Christmas shopping. He knew that he had found his mission. He would make many people happy before Christmas Eve.

The Chubby Cheek Angel

Strange things started to happen on the third of December. It was half past five and Mrs Huber-Haubner came back from a coffee afternoon with her friends. She tripped on her own doorstep and nearly fell over. Someone had put a shapeless package there, which in the darkness looked like a potato sack. Mrs Huber-Haubner switched on the light and unwrapped the parcel. There was a wooden figurine with wings, painted in red and blue, with a candle holder in its hands. An angel lamp that people used to hang on their walls. This item, however, was no antique but a rather clumsy copy. The head was far too big for the body, its hands were too large and the rosy-cheeked face was cracked by an awkward crooked smile. An exceptionally kitschy piece.

***

Mrs Huber-Haubner was not amused. Was this a prank, a mistake or really a genuine present? She took a closer look at the figure and noticed a tag tied to the hand. A shaky hand had written: "From Heaven Above to Earth I Come". Nothing else. Nothing about the sender, no greeting, no explanation.

To begin with, she picked up the phone and called all her friends and acquaintances, one after the other. Still, after two hours – while the dinner got burnt and Mr Huber-Haubner raged – she was no wiser. Nobody admitted to being the sender of the angel. What on earth should she do with it? Keep it in her house? Absolutely out of the question. Interior of glass, chrome and marble styled by a renowned designer would only accommodate a violet-green Vasarely and a black-and-white cat. Anything else would be a style faux pas.

Mrs Huber-Haubner did not need to think long. The lowest shelf in the linen closet was just right to stow away the ugly thing. She wrapped the figure up again, put it next to the no-more used Barchent sheets, closed the door and tried to forget the whole episode. She would probably have succeeded if it weren't for the crackle and rustle in the closet every night at half past five and if the cat hadn't stood there in front of the door with an arched back. Mrs Huber-Haubner went to check it out several times but there was nothing extraordinary to be seen. However, on the fourth day it looked to her as if the packaging paper might have moved a bit. In any case, the two large wooden candle-holding hands stretched out towards her. She quickly wrapped up the hands again and covered them with a stack of sheets, just to be sure. On the fifth day, at half past five, it rustled again. Mrs Huber-Haubner opened the closet and the chubby-cheeked face smirked at her, the crumpled packaging paper just next to it.

***

A creepy feeling came over Mrs Huber-Haubner. Had the cat been in the closet or had the cleaning lady messed around? It could not possibly be the case that the angel itself... Appalled at the thought, she shooed it away. "Pull yourself together, Marta, and be reasonable", she said to herself. Wooden angels are wooden angels and they cannot move. Period.

Nonetheless, a certain uneasiness remained. Hence, when the rustling turned into a silent singing on the sixth day, she made a decision: "It must go! Out of sight, out of mind!"

Straight away she put it in a box and took it out to the rubbish.

***

However, you cannot get rid of an angel so easily. Less than two hours later, the manager of the municipal street maintenance stood in front of the house door holding the cardboard box containing the smirking chubby-cheeked fella. He explained that he was very sorry that his team had nearly thrown this valuable piece into the garbage truck. That must clearly be an oversight. Would the lady please excuse this incident. "Alright," thought Mrs Huber-Haubner, "there must be other ways." She knew that the local business association would soon hold its traditional Christmas exhibition and that the organisers were looking for raffle prizes. That sealed the fate of the angel. Mrs Huber-Haubner cast a cold eye on the almost pleading smile of the angel, packed him neatly and took it to the collection point.

That should have put her at ease. However, driven by an unexplainable feeling, she went to visit the Christmas exhibition in the big hall of the hotel Krone on the 15th of December. "I really wonder whether it is still there," she thought. And indeed: there was the angel on the table of gifts, holding a red candle, in between a toaster and a vase, a pair of gloves in front of it and three bottles of wine behind it. A sight which is not uncommon at a raffle. All good. This was exactly what she had in mind. A boring housewife would receive it as a prize and put it on a boring wall of her stuffy and boring flat. Exactly so. That pig-ugly thing should be in a pig-ugly place. In the end, she had never ordered it, the thing had just landed at hers. Landed? "From Heaven Above to Earth I Come", flashed up in her mind. She felt a pang of guilt. Didn't it look somewhat sad? The chubby cheeks were hanging down. She rushed to the stand with Christmas decorations, bought three white candles for her designer chandelier and left the exhibition without looking back at the table of prizes.

The angel´s sad expression haunted her for a while, but soon other things required her full attention. Christmas was approaching and there were a thousand preparations to be done: last gifts to be bought, a Christmas tree to be decorated, a festive dinner to be planned. On the morning of the 25th she was busy stuffing the Christmas goose when the doorbell rang. There stood the President of the business association. "Congratulations and Merry Christmas," he exclaimed, "your entry ticket to the Christmas exhibition won the first prize in our raffle!" He cheerfully handed a shapeless package over to Mrs Huber-Haubner. "From Heaven Above to Earth I Come", was written on the attached note. The chubby-cheeked face was clearly visible through the silk paper, smiling triumphantly.